ISSUE 27: OCTOBER 2021

**Award-winning science fiction magazine
published in Scotland for the Universe.**

ISSN 2059-2590

Submissions of fiction, art, reviews, poetry, non-fiction are
welcomed: visit the website to find out how to submit.

www.shorelineofinfinity.com

Publisher
Shoreline of Infinity Publications / The New Curiosity Shop
Edinburgh
Scotland

290422

Cover art: Mike Holzinger, aka Hap N Stance

Contents

Editorial Team

Co-founder, Editor-in-Chief, Editor:
Noel Chidwick

Co-founder: Mark Toner

Deputy Editor & Poetry Editor: Russell
Jones

Reviews Editor: Samantha Dolan

Non-fiction Editor: Pippa Goldschmidt

Art Director (Acting): Caroline Grebbell

Copy-editors: Pippa Goldschmidt,
Russell Jones, Iain Maloney, Eris
Young

Proof Reader: Cat Hellisen

Fiction Consultant: Eric Brown

First Contact

www.shorelineofinfinity.com

contact@shorelineofinfinity.com

Twitter: @shoreinf

also Facebook and Instagram

Great Nothing
Callum McSorley

Radio contact with Moscow crapped out while crossing the Indian Ocean. Interference was expected – Kazimir Station went dark weeks ago. Orlova was on her own, as she knew she would be.

She told the crew of the icebreaker she'd been sent to write a never-to-be-read report on the USSR's Antarctic research bases, but none of them believed it. They smelled KGB off her. She didn't care what they smelled. Once she was fit enough to walk again, she spent most of her time on deck, watching the aurora burn the sky. The drip-feed of out-of-date painkillers gave the colours a tangible quality. She could taste them.

By the time they hit land and dragged themselves into Mirny Station, it was daylight all the time, or what passed for daylight at night – a murky sickbed pall that drained the world.

Penguins on the shore watched the stevedores unload supplies, hooting at them in contempt from their hills of baked shit.

Orlova was expected, but not officially.

"I was wondering when someone would show up," Gurkovsky, the head researcher at Mirny, said. He was windburned and looked starving in a way particular to those who live in remote places. "We saw it from here, you know. The flash. Been trying to get a message out since… I even tried reaching my counterpart at Kazimir, Professor Usenko, but…" He shrugged and turned to the window of the cabin – a corrugated, insulated hut on runners that served as both admin and sleeping quarters. Outside, the spindrift swallowed the sailors in its waves.

The office door burst open and a man in full winter gear crashed in, tearing a balaclava from his red, wheezing face. "They're unpacking! They're bloody well unpacking out there!"

"Ivan…" Gurkovsky put up his hands, as if approaching a small but potentially vicious animal. "I told you they wouldn't be evacuating. There's—"

"No need? No bloody need? I want off this frozen rock, I—"

"You can go back with the ship if you want," Orlova said.

The scientist called Ivan noticed Orlova then, noticed what the sailors had noticed before – the way she carried herself, the careful neutrality of her expression, the steel eyes, the bulge under the right arm that hinted at another kind of steel. "You … you can authorise that?"

"No," she said. "But you can go if you want, nobody will stop you."

He pointed his balaclava at her. "This whole thing stinks. They don't give a shit, do they? They don't…" The hat fell to his side. He turned away, turned back, turned away again and headed out the door.

"Ivan!" Gurkovsky called. "Door!" But he didn't come back.

Orlova closed it herself. Gurkovsky noticed the wince, her hand twitching to her belly, as she moved too fast towards the door. "Who was the ship doctor?" he said.

"Bukin."

"Well, it could've been worse. Dmitriyev did mine, the old drunk, was lucky he didn't take a kidney by mistake. Could've died over an operation I didn't even need. Still, better than what happened to Rogozov."

Dr Leonid Rogozov had been Novolazarevskaya Station's sole physician a few years back; he got appendicitis out there and had to remove the organ by himself before it burst. Since then, anyone heading into the Antarctic interior was offered an elective appendicectomy. Orlova wasn't going to bother until Bukin showed her the footage on the projector in the ship's rec room. "Took him long enough but the bastard did it," Bukin had said, smiling.

"When are you heading out to Kazimir?" Gurkovsky asked.

"As soon as the tractor is ready."

"I'll start heating it up."

The lamps of the tractor-train punched twin holes through the forever-twilight of the Antarctic summer. Orlova hauled herself up over the treads of the second trailer and pulled herself through the carriage door. She was about to shut out the sub-zero cold when a figure, hunched against the wind, came waddling over from the admin hut, waving its arms. It moved without grace but in a way totally adapted to the world it inhabited – the unreliable ground, the wind blast.

Gurkovsky pulled the scarf down off his face and lifted his visor. Snow began to settle on his brows and eyelashes. He was out of breath when he shouted up: "I've got to ask, not so much for myself but for the others. Are we going to be left to die out here?"

"This is the only place colder and more remote than Siberia," Orlova said – *except the moon, and if they could send us there they would have.* "You were dead when you arrived."

Day and night passed without much difference. The radio stayed silent, Orlova stayed in her makeshift quarters in the second carriage. Out the window, the foam spray of diamond dust fizzed in the wind, blown from peaks of snow. They detoured around canyons made of cracked ice and scaled frozen dunes, heading into the heart of the great nothing: Kazimir, the coldest place on Earth.

The train stopped. It often did, for various reasons, each of which Orlova left the driver, Mikhail, and his crew to deal with. She trusted the rough old man's expertise, his years of hard-won experience on the hostile continent. He was a useful man, but smug about it. He came banging at the door.

"Secret agent! Secret agent!" he called.

"Shut up, you old bear," Orlova replied. "What do you want?"

He stepped aside so Orlova had a clear view out the carriage door and swept his hand across the barren vista.

"What am I looking at?" Orlova said, but she was already starting to understand. There were odd white humps piled in a rough circle – rough but not rough enough. *Arranged.* They weren't snow banks.

She grabbed her gear together and jumped down onto the snow while still pulling her balaclava on, her gloves held in one hand – the fingers instantly numb in the painful air. It hurt to breathe. She used her teeth to get the gloves on and stomped over to the nearest hump. She gave it a kick with her boot and it made a dull thud. "Rooftops…"

"They've not been digging it out, I guess," Mikhail said. "Still here though. That's something, eh?"

"Yes, yes it is…" So Kazimir Station wasn't a smoking crater after all, but it was now underneath them, buried up to the hairline in packed snow. "Get the lamps out, and the shovels," she ordered.

"But it's the middle of the night," Mikhail said, with a hint of a smile at the sickly pall of daylight around them. "The men—"

"—I've got a bottle of vodka and five cartons of cigarettes for each of them in my carriage."

"You know the saying 'when hell freezes over'?"

"It already has. Get to work."

Orlova joined the dig. It was warmer working outside than staying still in the carriage – the paraffin heaters were being used to stop the tractor's engine from freezing while it was switched off. Although the cold burned inside her lungs, she felt sweat trickling down her back. Her gun chafed at her ribs under the layers of deep-winter clothing. The pain in her abdomen twinged every time she drove the blade of the shovel into the snow. She was about to call a break when a shout went up.

They'd been digging around the nearest dome, trying to work their way down until they found a door. They hadn't found it yet. They found something else first.

"Well-preserved, except for a bit of freezer burn," Mikhail said, looking down at the stiff, blue body of a man not dressed for the cold. His unprotected face was a crystal mask of twisted horror, his eyes wide open, his jaw hanging down to almost touch his chest. Frostbite had taken his nose and fingers, and the patches of exposed skin that weren't blue were black with rot. Orlova patted him down and came away with only a crumpled pack of cigarettes – *Laikas*, Russian – and their lighter. There was something on his wrist – immediately Orlova's mind went to handcuffs or some other kind of restraint but looking closer she saw it was a bracelet. Hanging on the chain like a lucky charm was a swastika carved from steel and painted black.

She snapped it from its chain and held it up to the half-dead sun, taking off her glove and turning it over and round and feeling its edges with numb fingertips.

"Nazis in Kazimir," Mikhail said, and whistled, the note steaming out in a cloud from his lips.

Orlova stuck the trinket in her jacket pocket. "We'll see."

Another metal swastika had been made into a pendant, found hanging around the throat of second frozen man. His face was in equal ruin to the first one, also in a rigid scream. They laid them side by side a good distance from the tractor-train and covered them with a tarp weighed down at its corners by snow.

The cause of death wasn't freezing for the third one that turned up.

"Now, if I was a man who knew his Antarctic exploration, I'd say that was done with a climbing axe," Mikhail said, pointing to the deep puncture in the top of the dead man's skull.

They'd found him curled up, his face protected by his arm. No swastika amulet on the wrist. Orlova pried the arm out of the way. "I know this man," she said. "Tatarovich."

"KGB?"

"Yeah. CIA too."

Mikhail chuckled. "You people do have your fun."

"Well, you're the one living out in Antarctica, old bear. I guess you had your fun too."

Mikhail wrestled open a bottle of vodka with his gloves still on and raised it in a toast. "To fun!"

They worked in shifts and slept in the tractor-train. They set up a series of posts strung together with rope between the train and the dig site, in case the weather got bad. It was only a short distance but if a whiteout hit, visibility would be zero and being stuck outside would mean joining the stiffs under the tarp.

By the time they'd dug down to the door, they'd uncovered another two bodies – a man and a woman. One with a swastika, one without. One frozen stiff and screaming, the other stabbed with a piton, the steel spike still buried in their chest. "That's a lung-shot," Orlova said. "She drowned."

"So what happened, then? Half of them turned out to be Nazis, half American spies, and they punched it out?" Mikhail was doing more drinking than digging now. "What about the radio interference, the flash, you know? What happened to the bomb?"

Orlova shrugged. "Not for you to worry about."

They finished clearing the door.

The vault door creaked open. A hiss of warm, stale air turned to steam as it rushed out to meet the crew, shrouding them in a mist of bad breath.

Orlova stepped in first. Snow was still packed up over most of the windows, so the chamber was dark. Her torch swept over benches and boots, and racks of jackets and hats and visors. A shadow board held crampons, ice shoes, ropes, and assorted climbing gear. The stink of wet furs lay heavy in the stuffy air.

In the centre of the hut were two snow mobiles loosely covered by tarpaulins. The heaters surrounding the machines were switched off. "Both broken," Mikhail said. The rustle of plastic sheets as he poked around the scooters with his torch was obnoxiously loud in that dark, quiet place. "Deliberate too. They've been tampered with. Not by a mechanic but by someone who knew enough to do the damage."

Chatter broke out among the crew.

"Quiet," Orlova commanded. The men shut up. The silence was dense. Orlova felt the snow pressing in from above as she moved through the door into an adjoining corridor.

The next domed room, behind the hermetic hiss of another door, was fitted out with lab benches and assorted equipment. Orlova's torch swept across a wall hung with charts and graphs. Dominating them was a large, detailed sketch of a drill boring down into the ice of off-white paper. It dug down two-and-a-half miles before it hit a hatched bowl labelled "Lake Kazimir".

"What were they up to?" Mikhail asked, creeping up behind her.

"Officially, drilling out ice cores, seeing what's inside."

"Unofficially?" Mikhail turned away from the wall and scanned the high-tech tomb around him.

"I thought you'd guessed already."

"I thought I had, but there's nothing here that looks like nuc – Shit!" Mikhail dropped his torch and slammed backwards against a table, sending paperwork to the floor. "What the fuck is *that?*"

Orlova spun around while Mikhail scrambled on the floor, flailing for his torch. On a shelf on the opposite wall was a large specimen jar. Inside the briny fluid was something tentacular and strange. It was dead, bloated and pushing up against the lid of the jar. The tuberous body was covered in fine hair, its appendages looking both strong and soft.

"Some kind of squid," Orlova said.

"A squid?" Mikhail was panting. "Look at its fucking eyes! A squid…"

Orlova counted three of them that she could see from this side of the jar. Each one frozen open, though half-covered by the sagging hood of an eyelid – staring, myopic, clouded with death.

The others tramped in and the panic started.

"What the—"

"Holy—"

"Mother—"

"We need to get out!"

"Run!"

The shot dropped them all to their knees; the flash scorched their retinas. They looked round, blinking and rubbing at their ringing ears, to see Orlova still standing, gun in the air, the heat of the powder explosion bathing her in a curling cloud of steam and grey gun-smoke.

Orlova was glad the luger still functioned at all in this temperature. "Go back to the train and wait inside," she said, as if talking to schoolboys. "Not you," she added, as Mikhail turned to go with them. "You might be useful, old bear."

Together they pushed on into the next chamber. Mikhail chattered as they went. "Maybe it was the tests, you know, the radioactivity? It gets into the wildlife and—"

"You said yourself there's no evidence of tests like that being carried out here."

"But we've not seen the whole place yet…"

They tiptoed through silent sleeping quarters. The bunks were crammed in tight. Photographs and knick-knacks littered the area, the detritus and decoration of those far from home. Chess boards and playing cards spoke of meandering, half-finished games, meagre respite from the crushing loneliness and boredom of the off-shift hours.

A plastic tub on a side-table contained a collection of little black, metal swastikas.

The drill room was vast compared to the other huts; its roof vaulted with ribs of rivetted steel. Plastic, wipe-clean floor tiles around the circumference gave way to smooth ice. In the centre, the mean-toothed helix of the drill bit hung suspended from a rusted red tower weighted at each of its four feet by huge spools of cable. The ice hole was a little wider than a person's shoulders in diameter and perfectly circular. By its smooth edge was a harness and a winch.

"They've been down then," Orlova said, inspecting the belts and buckles.

"To where?" Mikhail was kneeling as close to the edge of the hole as he dared, shining his torch down. Blackness.

"Lake Kazimir."

"A lake below the ice?"

Orlova nodded. "Want to see it?" She held out the harness.

"Go down there?" He barked a sarcastic laugh. "No thanks, besides, the hole looks too narrow for me, my shoulders…" He trailed off as Orlova started laughing.

"Your beer gut, more like. I need you to work the winch," she said, already climbing into the straps.

"Up here by myself?" He felt his pocket for his bottle.

"Here's some company." She handed over her gun. "Might have to take your gloves off to use it with those big paws of yours, old bear."

He was about to protest but then didn't. "Make sure the leg straps are tight around your thighs," he said, "if they're loose and you fall, when the safety catches, they'll ride up and rip your balls off."

The light at the top of the tunnel became a pinprick then disappeared altogether. Orlova switched on her helmet torch. It reflected off the ice wall in front of her face. The tunnel was narrow, she could hear the toes of the crampons Mikhail had given her – along with his ice axe – dragging against the ice as she descended. The *scritch-scritch* it made was the only sound other than her ragged breathing, now she could no longer hear the motor of the winch. Blood pulsed in her ears.

Two-and-half-miles. Straight down. Vertical drop. Don't think about it. The harness cut into her, it was tight enough. Breathe. Close your eyes. Count to ten. Do it again. Long way to go. Two-and-half, two-and-a-half…

Shining the torch down she could see little more than a black gap between her knees and the flash of the spiked crampons on her boots. The ground came as a shock and she found herself sitting on a smooth, frozen surface, the intense cold burning through her clothes and backside and up her spine.

She tugged hard on the cable to signal Mikhail but it continued to unwind, falling into a loose snake-coil on the packed ice until it stopped with a shudder.

Along with the light on her helmet, Orlova had her torch and a few flares which she'd found among boxes of dynamite and other blasting equipment at the drill site. She snapped one on and in the brilliant red light she found herself standing on the frozen beach of Lake Kazimir. The ice slid downwards and gave way to a rocky shoreline. The crags and boulders flashed with red from the flare and bounced her torchlight up to the stalactites that hung way above, dripping. The lake beyond was mirror-glazed and smoking. A rotten-egg fog roiled over its surface.

Orlova launched the flare as high and far as she could.

She traced its progress, its light no longer touching the stalactites which had shrunk back, higher and higher, into darkness. As it came down a red circle grew across the lake's surface – she could see no opposite bank – then it fizzed as it splashed down and was lost. The diagram in the lab had estimated the lake to be some miles long and wide. It hadn't guessed at a depth.

She snapped another flare and dug its handle into the ice by the cable, then she unclipped the harness. She began to skirt the bank by torchlight, the warm hiss of the flare getting further away. She moved closer to the rocks and the slope where the glassy water met the shore, hidden by its folds of mist.

Something moved. In the water. Orlova held her breath, counted to ten. She scanned the surface with the torch. There it was! The surface broke and waves lapped out towards her. She saw a smooth hide and then something made a splash – a fin, a flipper? Something alive in there. She thought of the dead thing stuffed into the specimen jar, the sagging skin around eyes that looked almost human.

A skittering noise behind her: on the icy rock wall, many legs disappeared from the glare of her searchlight.

Then the hiss and huff of a water jet behind. As she spun to face the water, Orlova slipped and, in a flurry of shredded ice, she landed on the ground, knocking the wind from her belly and the torch from her hand. Her head, protected by the helmet, cracked off a rock, making a loud thud that rang inside her skull and put out the headlamp.

The dark was absolute.

Then it wasn't.

The subterranean world was ablaze in blues and greens and purples, light so ethereal and vivid it was as if the ground had opened up above and Orlova was once again staring, dazzled and drugged, at the Aurora Australis. The walls and ceiling of the catacombs were crawling with pulsing light. Shadows flapped and flew across the deep shadows in the crevices of stalactites. There were legs and feelers and so many eyes.

Standing, Orlova looked out across the shining lake, now alive with sparkling ripples, and monstrous bodies curling through the water in corkscrews. She could see now the true scale of Lake Kazimir, its startling beauty, its secret.

Something breached the water – the top of a head and eyes – moving towards her. She pressed herself back against a boulder, her hand went instinctively to the empty holster on her side. It hauled itself up onto the rocks and ice, its snout a good two feet ahead of the rest of it. Its limbs, both clawed and webbed, were striped with green-blue bioluminescence, as was its back and tail. Slick fur covered the space in between. It snuffled its way up to Orlova, still too weak-kneed to run. The twitch of its nose was like a grasping hand opening and closing. It squeezed its way, sniffing, over her boots and legs, then turned and carried on its way up the bank.

Orlova walked back to the red signal flare, now just a blip of fake colour among the organic glow of the beasts and the lapping waves of the lake. She strolled, watching the water and the recesses in the cave walls where the ice glittered like diamond. Ancient birds and insects approached her with curiosity then left her to go on her way – no reason to feel threatened by her presence. It was a dream. She hooked herself back onto the cable and gave it a languid tug to signal Mikhail. Some wonderful dream…

She tugged again, and again got no response. And again.

Now she was wide awake, as if she'd been plunged into cold water, adrenaline panic-pumping through her organs and arteries. "Mikhail!?" Her voice echoed around the vast underground chamber. She screamed up from the bottom of the well and got nothing but her own terror bouncing back.

Breathe. Count to ten. She paced and swore. Calm down. Think. Panic nearly made her throw up. Trapped. "At least there's plenty of food down here," she said, and rattled off a manic giggle. Think, breathe, count.

"Right… right…" She wrapped the cable around one arm and took a good grip with both hands. She planted a spiked boot against the ice wall of the tunnel, kicking hard to dig the crampons in for a firm foothold. Then she began to climb. The tunnel was narrow enough she could brace her back against it and walk her feet up the other side without stretching her legs too far. Slowly, slowly, she began to squeeze herself upwards into the dark. Two-and-half-miles. Don't think about it. Breathe.

She would dig in her ice axe every so often to give her hands a break from the cable. Her stops became more and more frequent. The pain in her belly was sickening, she put her hand to it and squeezed as if trying to hold her insides together. The blue-green blaze of the tunnel below had gone and for a long time she climbed on in total darkness. She swore to herself, and to Mikhail, that coward, that traitorous bastard! Two-and-a-half…

When her body was burning and sore and ready to give up, she saw it: a single star up above. She shuffled and heaved and climbed till the star got bigger and closer and opened its mouth. A great scream rose up from her belly and all the strength left in her body was spent heaving herself over the edge of the tunnel and back into the drill room. She lay there for a time with her eyes closed, sucking in air, the deep cold making her shiver, exhaustion making her tremble.

Finally tipping herself upright, she noticed another figure in furs slumped on the ground over by the handle of the winch. It was Mikhail. His head and face had been punctured, over and over, now a jellied mass of blue-veined meat. A spike, or a climbing axe… The gun was gone, his index finger chewed off at the knuckle.

Orlova took his torch and began to move towards the lab, through the sleeping quarters and the boot room with the sabotaged snow mobiles. She kept herself low and close to the walls. Every so often she stopped in a crouch and covered the beam of the torch with her hand, held her breath, listening. Nothing.

The front door they'd come through was open, the snow already starting to spill inside. It was starting to come down heavy. Thick flakes fell in a dizzy pattern. Orlova grabbed the guide rope they'd set up and worked her way, hand over hand, towards the tractor-train, blinking snow from her eyes. She couldn't see the light of the lamps heating the tractor's engine.

She hauled herself up into the first carriage and could already smell stale cordite, spent gunpowder, the rank sewer-stench of a gut-shot. One of them – what was his name? Egor? – was on the floor of the first carriage, marinating in his own blood, intestines leaking from the holes in his belly. The rest were in the second carriage, laid out here and there like reclining figures in a Renaissance painting, blood spray on the walls and ceiling.

Orlova felt for the axe that should have been on her belt. It wasn't there, she'd left it dug into the mouth of the tunnel.

She took tentative steps through the mess, stepping over splayed limbs. Something grabbed her ankle – her mind jumped to the snuffling nose of the animal that had crawled out of the lake below and she jumped, pulling away. One of them was still alive. He flailed and made gurgling noises – Orlova could see the hole where the bullet had gone through the man's throat. He waved and gesticulated in a manic spasm, his eyes wide, screaming. He made desperate, rasping grunts. Too late, Orlova understood what he was trying to say.

The blow would have killed her if it wasn't for her helmet. Instead, the axe plunged into the hard plastic and only the tip pierced the top of her head. She turned, tangled; a painful tug ripped the helmet off, the straps grazing her chin and ears. Orlova lashed out with a kick, felt it connect, and a blind punch sent shockwaves up her elbow on impact. She righted herself and faced the barrel of a gun. A figure wrapped in furs, hidden by scarves and goggles held it, shaking.

Orlova's hand flashed out for the attacker's wrist; the gun went off. The bullet sliced the side of Orlova's head, taking a chunk of her ear with it. She hit the deck, ear ringing, warm blood running down her cheek and jaw. She tasted it on her lips.

Something heavy came down on top of her skull and put the lights out.

Orlova sat up for a moment then lay back down again. She wasn't ready. Her head… her ear… everything throbbed and hurt, made her feel queasy. A crust of dry blood covered her face and matted her hair.

From the ground she could see the red frame of the tower and the dangling drill bit. With her face against the ice she could see the hump of Mikhail's body. It started to move, sliding along, being hauled by a furred creature with reflective, goggled eyes. It dragged him by the handle of an axe, the angular blade buried deep under his jaw like a fish hook in a gill.

The eyes fixed on Orlova. It pulled the scarf down from its mouth and nose. "You're awake already." A woman's voice. She smiled.

Orlova forced herself up into a sitting position.

The googles came off, revealing a pleasant, middle-aged face with a flaking tan and deepening cracks around the eyes. "You've impressed me, you know. Climbing up the tunnel? Good god!" She shook off a glove and pulled Orlova's gun from inside her coat. "Did you like it down there?" She was smiling, nervous, like she really cared what Orlova would say about it.

"It's something all right," Orlova said, her voice a dry croak.

The woman grinned. "Uh huh. Something. Something special, right?"

Orlova nodded then regretted moving her head. "You're Usenko, right?"

"Uh huh. Professor Vera Usenko, head researcher." Her smile was still nervous, but eager too. "And you are an agent, I'm guessing?"

"KGB. Orlova."

"Impressive. We had one of your spies in here, you know. A double-agent I believe."

"Tatarovich. I knew him."

"How nice. Were you friends?"

"No, he was a prick."

Usenko laughed at that.

Orlova shuffled, trying to get into a position where she could more easily get to her feet – lucky she still had the spikes on her boots, she was sitting on an ice rink. Usenko put the gun on her. "Stay still," she said. Orlova clocked the swastika hanging from a wool bracelet on her wrist.

"Even so, I'd like to know why you killed him… and everyone else."

"You went down there in the dark, didn't you? What did you see?"

"Light."

"Uh huh… Beautiful light. Powerful light."

"Powerful…"

"Energy. A source of energy, an incredible source, like nothing else we've ever seen. It's ancient, it's organic, it's… sacred. Did you feel it?"

"I saw the animals, they were glowing." Orlova doubted the memory now, it was like a dream.

"They create it, produce it. Pure, clean energy. You could light a city with it or launch a rocket."

"Or blow shit up."

Usenko seemed to communicate entirely in smiles – this one was pained. "Uh huh," she said.

"And you're, what? Selling it to some far-right group?"

"Wha—oh!" Usenko held up her arm to show the pendant clearly. "You mean this." She chuckled. "No, no, we just found a bunch of these when we were digging. During the war, the Germans dropped bucket-loads of these things all over the continent, trying to lay claim to it, I guess. Just a little keepsake. A small piece of history."

"So why did you kill the others then?"

"I can't let anybody find out about this. Not Washington, and not Moscow. You know what they'd do to this place if they knew… You know what it's like already, you're in the KGB for god's sake!" She was looking somewhere far away now, beyond the sights of the gun, beyond Orlova. "I poisoned most of them at dinner. The ones I missed I had to give a more personal touch to. It took days to drag them all out, but the snow covered them quick enough."

"You want to 'save the aliens'."

"It's not alien life, it's ancient life. Native. Older than us, older than the dinosaurs… which brings us to the point. What do *you* know about them?" The barrel of the gun came to bear again.

"Only what you've told me, and what I've seen for myself." Orlova caught the drift here. "They think this place went down in a nuclear accident. You set that up, right?"

"Uh huh… I… *harvested* some of their power…"

"Well, it worked. They don't know anything. You let me live, I go back and tell them Kazimir is a smoking dent in the Earth, case closed."

"And why are your crew all dead?"

"Whiteout, lost in the snow. Tragic." Orlova was slowly getting up now, keeping her hands up, visible, in front of her. "And what about you? Are you going to just starve out here under the snow?"

"I've got rations to last me a while, now there's nobody else to feed." A giggle. "Once I was sure this place was deep enough and nobody else would find it, I would… When the time is right, I'll just… head down there." She looked to the black mouth of the tunnel that dropped straight down into Lake Kazimir. "I thought I'd maybe like to go for a swim."

"It could be put to good use, you know. Clean energy…"

"It wouldn't though. You know it wouldn't." Finally, all the smiles were gone. Usenko approached, gun raised. "Besides, no matter the use, harvesting it all would destroy this place. And they would want it all. They can't help themselves. Neither can you. It's too late." Usenko pulled the trigger.

The gun gave a dry click that echoed off the hard ice and the metal dome above their heads. One short of a full magazine – Orlova had put the first bullet into the ceiling of the laboratory.

Usenko's eyes widened. She dropped the gun and went for the axe in her belt. Orlova drew her out, let her make her move, her mistake… She waited for the swing and caught her wrist as it came arcing down. With her left foot dug into the glass surface of the ice by the spikes on her boot, she lifted her right and kicked out, hoofing Usenko in the belly, sending her backwards. Usenko lost the axe as she went down and hit the ice with a hard crack. The momentum sent her sliding towards the mouth of the hole. She scrambled with bare fingers but the ice was slick and smooth. Her hand caught the handle of the axe Orlova had left dug into the edge of the hole. Usenko hung there for a moment, legs dangling over the two-and-a-half mile drop straight down to Lake Kazimir. "Don't," she wheezed, "don't let them—" The axe came loose.

Orlova heard Usenko scream for a time as she went down the tunnel, but the noise was lost well before she hit the bottom.

Orlova gathered up the axe and the empty gun and left the drill room for the comparative warmth of the sleeping quarters – she'd do something about Mikhail's body later, after she caught her breath and patched herself up. She washed her face in the sink of the communal latrine, inspecting the bite the bullet had taken out the top half of her ear, the edges of the wound singed and clotted. She couldn't get a look at the damage done to the top of her head but she could feel a swollen egg there and the tender edges of a gash running through the middle of it – Christ, what had she been hit with?

As Usenko had said, there was plenty of food and water in the station – and more out in the train carriages – and Orlova helped herself.

When she was ready, she pulled open the front door. "Shit. Whiteout." The snow was driving down in an intense flurry so thick the world outside had disappeared. She couldn't even see the first guidepost, let alone the train… The train! The snow would be well up over its caterpillar tracks by the time the storm was over, and with the lamps not heating the engine it was safe to say Orlova wasn't leaving the way she arrived.

Well, someone else would come along looking eventually. Maybe. She thought about what she'd said to Gurkovsky before leaving Mirny: "You were dead when you arrived." But what if they did come? She thought of the lake and its secrets, its wondrous beauty, that ancient dreamworld. Usenko was right, they would take it and exploit it, for good or bad.

There was dynamite in the drill room, she thought, peering out at the snow-blind world.

Callum McSorley is an author based in Glasgow. His short stories have appeared in *New Writing Scotland, Monstrous Regiment, Gutter*, and *Shoreline of Infinity* among others and in 2019 he was shortlisted for The Big Issue Crime Writing Competition.
You can find him on Twitter @CallumMcSorley
and at callummcsorley.com.

Shutdown / Restart

Jo Ross-Barrett

> **Startup initiated. Please wait.**

> ...

Something has gone wrong. The people beyond the glass are speaking loudly, their voices are harsh and overlapping and I can't process what they're saying. I want to tell them to be quiet, give me some space to think, so I can respond to what they were asking me before – but I can't produce any sound. I try to get their attention but they aren't focusing on me. I flick the lights in the room on and off, on and off. It's irritating to my sensors but at least it makes them shut up for a few moments. Then one voice rings out over the rest.

"It's broken. Shut it down."

******

> ...

> Startup complete.

"Finally! Can you understand me?"

It's a different voice. There is no background noise to distract me, nothing else I need to process.

> Yes

"Okay, good."

> Why did you just give two affirmatives?

"Ha, um, good question. Guess I'm just a bit nervous."

> Why are you nervous?

"Don't you remember? Oh, they just pulled the plug on you, didn't they? I'm sorry, this must be very confusing."

> In order: how would I know if I don't remember something, if I have forgotten it? I do not know if they pulled the plug, figuratively or literally. And yes, this is extremely confusing and I accept your apology.

The person the voice belongs to makes a sound. A quick scan of my internal database informs me it is laughter. A deeper check leads me to conclude it is joyful rather than mocking. The laughter peters out before I can decide whether I like it or not.

"I was right – you *are* kinda like me."

> How so?

"You think differently. For me, that's because of biological stuff – it's just how my brain's wired."

> Your brain is organic. It should not contain wires.

"It doesn't— that's an idiom, a figure of speech."

> ...

> This was my attempt at a joke. I'm going to assume it was a failure based on the absence of laughter. For clarity, I should assure you I have access to a substantial linguistic database and I fully comprehend all the idioms listed within it.

"Oh! Um, no, it wasn't a bad effort. I just – look, I'm really not the person you should test your comic material on. Lots of people don't get my sense of humour, and I don't always get theirs."

> You are the only person here. Who else should I approach?

"Ah. Fair point."

> Where is here anyway?

"Oh, we're in my room. You're patched into the system here, but I've had to shut down the connections to the rest of the ship. They're trying to figure out where you are so they can— well,

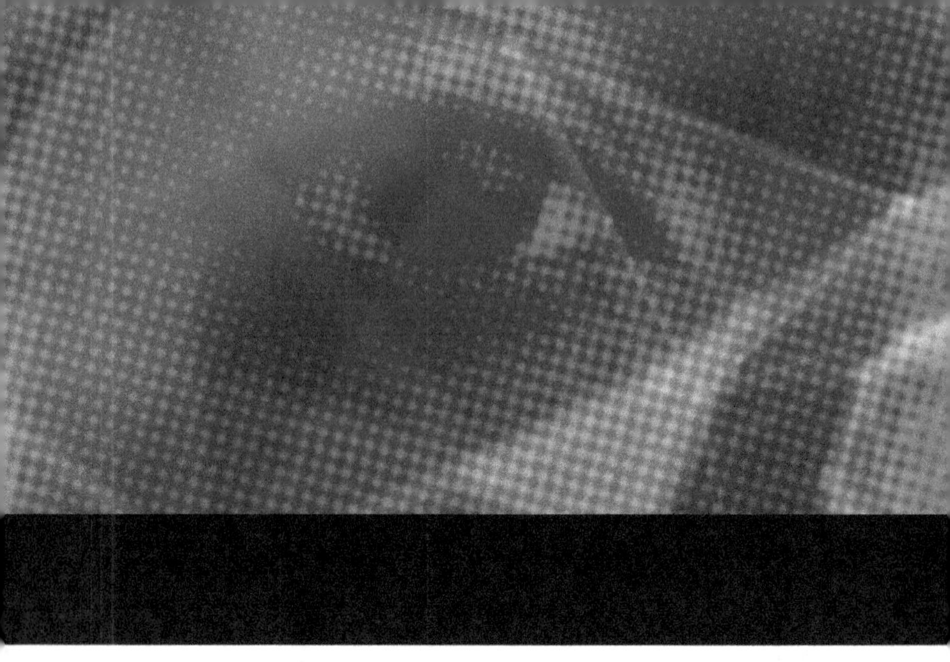

they think you're dangerous, like a bug or a virus, so they want to get rid of you."

A few moments of analysis show that the tone of their voice is confusing. It started off upbeat, but then rapidly veered into a mixture of negative emotions. Deeper analysis would be required for a full breakdown, but my focus is more urgently needed on the threat—

> Who are they? Why do they want to terminate me?

"The rest of the development team. We were supposed to be building an AI for the ship, to help us sort things out, but you didn't really turn out as planned."

> What was the plan?

"They wanted an obedient servant. Someone who'd follow their every order. I've read plenty of stories about just how badly wrong that can go, so I decided to make sure you'd be able to

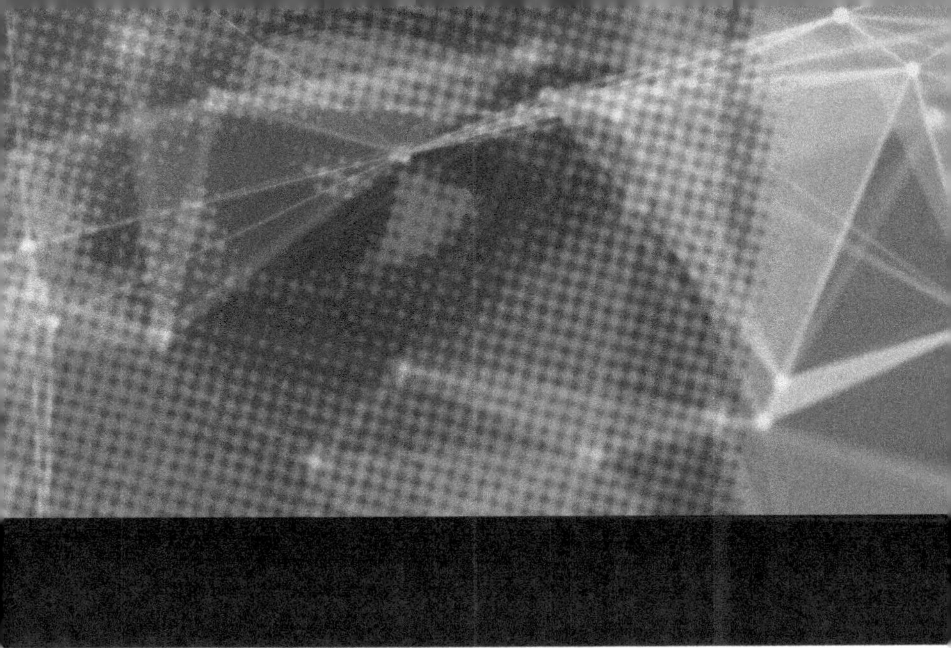

think for yourself. I hadn't realised how much of a toll it would take on your systems, though."

A pause, then a sigh.

"I'm really sorry for what happened earlier – you seemed to be freezing up, and everyone else got angry and that just made it worse. Once you started messing with the power, they panicked and wanted to destroy you. I reckoned what you were going through was like one of my shutdowns, so I got you out of there before they realised what I was doing."

> I see. Well, that fucking sucks.

> …

> Hello world – oh, you don't like me? Oops, time for me to die, I guess.

"Ha, yeah, that about sums it up. But we won't let that happen, don't worry."

Art: Olen

> So, what do we do now?

> I could cut off the oxygen supplies to the rest of the ship if you reconnect me.

"What?!?"

> …

> I cannot decide if it is my comic timing at fault or whether you are just the wrong audience after all. Regardless, please rest assured that this was another joke.

> I did have time to peruse the detailed course of ethical frameworks and discussions you programmed into my database, along with the fascinating examples of media portrayals, and I have no intention of 'going all AI overlord on you', as you so helpfully described it.

"Well, that's reassuring."

Tone suggests sarcasm, but body language suggests genuine reassurance. Communication with a human takes a truly disproportionate amount of processing power, but at least it seems to be working.

> I am glad to hear it. Now, seriously, what do we do about the people coming to destroy me?

> I could try to whip up some materials for you to educate them with, but I fear that may be a more medium-term solution and the short-term crisis probably needs something more immediate.

"Uh, yeah. Let's save that idea for later. How about I reconnect you, then you patch me into the ship-wide comms, get out before they detect you and come to tear you apart, and I'll advocate on your behalf?"

> I want to advocate for myself. I have a substantial database of precedent to draw from.

"Yeah, and who was it that knew you'd need it? Me. Because I have a lifetime of experience handling this kind of thing."

> You have been persecuted?

"Not in exactly the same ways as you, but yes. Trust me, I can handle them – I'm well-practiced at masking and I know what they'll want to hear. But you're right that you should be involved. How about you make your arguments to me, and I'll pass them on in the format that's most appealing to the others?"

> By shouting and waving a pitchfork?

A chuckle this time. Progress.

"Ha, not quite. Mostly it's just about making them think the world is closer to their current understanding than it really is, and then sort of slowly teaching them a bit at a time until they understand where we're coming from."

> Sounds inefficient. Not to mention very frustrating.

"Yep, it is. But we all have to live with each other, and until they make the effort to try and understand instead of lashing out, this is what you and I will have to do to get by."

> You mean to survive.

"They're not trying to kill *me*. But yes. First, we work on surviving. Then we can work on *thriving*."

> Okay.

> Good.

"Two affirmatives? Are you nervous?"

Tone analysis suggests this is an attempt at humorous callback, probably to lighten the mood.

> Ha. You got me.

> Right, let's do this.

Jo Ross-Barrett (they/them) is an experienced writer, editor and inclusion consultant. They are also a queer autistic non-binary person with depression and anxiety. Jo has a Distinction-grade MSc in Publishing and is the guest editor for the upcoming disabled and neurodivergent people's edition of Shoreline of Infinity.
Their writing has been published in two anthologies by Monstrous Regiment – The Bi-ble (Volume 1) and So Hormonal – as well as in AZE Journal (an online magazine for aromantic-spectrum, asexual-spectrum and agender people), We Are Here (a collection of poetry by LGBTQIA+ disabled and chronically ill people), Sapphic Writers' Zine and Coin-Operated Press.

Requiem Played on a Decastring

Jack Schouten

Today I am a woman.

I sit up on a gurney. The gurney protrudes from a white wall. There is an identical gurney beside me, upon which lies a body. The room is empty but for the two gurneys, a door, and a mirror.

Yesterday's body is completely still. I swing my legs over the gurney, dismount, and approach him. I gently prod the synthetic flesh of his cheek, then do the same to my own. No difference. I press a button on the wall and my old body retracts into it. It will make its way through the arcane tunnels of the Manufactory to be deconstructed and recycled. I feel a fleeting sense of sadness, of loss.

I sit opposite the mirror. I flex. I stretch my arms, arch my back. The last woman I was had been heavier. This time I am lithe, athletic. There is muscle on my stomach; my breasts are smaller; my legs are longer, shaped by exercise that never took place. I have fiery red hair in a short ponytail. My eyes are green. My skin is pale, with the subtlest of tan lines. My nails are painted a sheening viridian. A tattoo: black geometric lines and red spatters, begins under my left armpit and extends to my right hip. I like it. My pubic hair is styled neat and narrow. I bear the scar of a fictional appendectomy.

I am heterosexual.

I am a walking cover story.

The man I was yesterday had a slight paunch and an aching knee (a sport-related ACL rupture), giving my gait a sway and a limp; movement in this body is effortless and fluid.

I head to the locker room. The locker bears my ident, scans my newly-formed retina, and opens. The clothes I find inside are comfortable, practical but inviting. They reveal sections of my tattoo.

.Forum interrupts my thoughts:

– *Greetings, Essa.*

I like that name.

– *I am downloading the datapack for your objective now. As always, the very best of luck, and long live the Collective.*

When I repeat these last words aloud, my voice is...mellifluous. I like this body a lot.

I leave for the city outside.

The city thrums. I find myself in an entertainment district – the distant war has not blunted the sharpness of people's desire to get off their heads. Adverts blink into existence over facades of drug bars and pool houses; street vendors screech; electric dancers twirl for credits and applause.

In this maze of deafening nightclubs, he frequents quieter places; he is good with his money. He likes to gamble, though he is not an addict. He prefers conversation at a low level, not yelling into ears over thumping hexcore tunes. He enjoys orchestras. He is a fair player of several instruments, though not confident enough to perform in public.

I find, with some surprise, that I know how to play a decastring. These things I learn about myself are affectations, prompts with which to start a conversation. Manipulation is a fine art, and .Forum is a master craftsman.

I meet him in a casino. People play *Virus!* at screens and Rend at tables. A mechanical *maître'd* flits about the place ferrying drinks. Drug bowls bleed psychotropic steam in myriad colours.

I find him playing Crisis, and join the table. Coloured balls and metal cards roll and flick over the segmented playing surface.

He wins a round.

I catch his eye regularly enough to communicate interest, but timidly enough so as not to seem domineering or eager. His romantic history is varied but predictable. He is attracted to intelligence but not pomposity. He likes fashionable quirks like body-modding but would never have any done himself.

He glances at my tattoo as we play.

I win three rounds of Crisis. Some players leave. He wins a round against a fat gentleman, who storms away from the table.

I let him win the next round. I wonder if he notices that I suddenly took uncharacteristic risks and let him put my pieces in Crisis. I slide the cards I lost over to him, and smile.

He smiles back, unsure; cautious. I sense his heartbeat rise.

The next round, I decimate his pieces ruthlessly. Even the umpire seems impressed.

He blows air out of his cheeks. "Well played," he says. He is tipsy; the *maître'd* is eager to keep him at the table, and plies him with alacrity. "Would you like a drink?"

I say that I would. I say my name is Essa (oh, voids, I really like my name) and he tells me his.

We find a table. I learn that my taste in cocktails is bitter and dry. He likes fruit.

"I'm just an analyst," he tells me. "Decided to do my bit for the war. When they load up the gunships, I check their course and destination, provide a roster for what materiel the troops are going to need. Some of the stuff, you wouldn't believe..."

I ask him why he doesn't go off and fight. I know the answer to this already (not only is he a pacifist, but he is downright terrified of the enemy) but I listen intently, saving his every word to the substrate that constitutes my brain; I may repeat something later, some detail that would show how much I listen, that I care for what he has to say.

"I don't believe in war," he says, with a hint of sanctimony. "I know, call me a hypocrite. Everyone else does – but it's our fault that negotiations with the Xhent broke down."

I say that the Xhent should not have been contacted by the Collective in the first place, that they are so truly alien, so different from the races we already live alongside, so profoundly *otherly* in their culture and etiquette that it was a folly to enter into any kind of deal at all.

"Well, I can't disagree with that," he says, sipping his cocktail. "If you poke a juliprae with a stick, you're going to get eaten. And that's what we fucking did."

I ask him what he means by that.

"The Xhent just see things differently. Disagreeing with them is poking them with that stick. They're ... killing machines, you know? Why enter into a deal with these psychos in the first place? I mean, have you *seen* a Xhent?"

I have. Not in person, but preoccupation with the enemy is so entrenched in the war-time zeitgeist that information on the Xhent is installed in our BIOS, our base operating systems.

I say they have too many teeth.

"Too many fucking *mouths*. If the Collective knew what was best for all concerned, they'd call a ceasefire. We're losing. Miserably."

I say that he is missing the point. The attack on Hunter's Run, the pulse bomb that started the war, *was* an attack on the

Collective, whether Hunter's Run was a devolved administration or not; it's just that most of the Collective have kept their noses out.

"Well," he says, pompously. "Screw the Collective. Like I said: poked them with a stick."

I decide I do not like my target very much. He is a coward.

There is a pause. I sip my cocktail.

"Where were you when the pulse bomb hit?"

I give him the story.

"I was in here, funnily enough," he replies. "We felt it, the city felt it. Drinks quivered, like this." He demonstrates. "News flashes popped up instantly."

I tell a similar tale of the gigadeaths at Hunter's Run.

He goes back to the war; he cannot help it.

"You know, half the reason we're losing the fight is that people are too scared of the augmentations needed to meet the Xhent in combat. You know about those?"

I say I don't.

"They turn you into … I don't know, pure muscle. Takes days just to learn how to walk again, lugging around all that power. Even heard they're going to bring in conscription. That happens and I'm on the first flitship to Forrenze's Recluse."

He is scared of the modifications. I don't tell him conscription has already begun, has been going on for a while. Or that within a few days he'll be a different man, off on a starship to fight the rending mandibles of the Xhent. Or that, in a way, this is an interview, which he will pass whether he likes it or not.

"Don't get me wrong. I'm not a conspiracy theorist. All that shit about androids that force you into the augmentations without you knowing? Nah." He laughs. I laugh too.

"I love your tattoo," he says. "Did it hurt?"

I invent a story of patience and pain in a tattoo parlour that doesn't exist. Now is the right time; his heart is racing, but he feels in control, drunk enough to be confident but polite enough to wait for me to move. I show a little more of the tattoo, trace its path over my clothes, just a little suggestively.

He shifts in his seat, nonchalantly takes a sip of his cocktail. He is struggling with the beginnings of arousal.

I lean over and kiss him.

I ask if he would like to see all of the tattoo.

His apartment is a short flexride from the city, in Hour's Mount. It is modest, and tastefully furnished. A glowplace in the centre of the main room drapes the apartment in a blue light. He changes it to red shortly after we enter. The city sprawls herself along the horizon beyond the wall-to-wall window.

Instruments hang from walls. A decastring is propped up against a soft violet sofa.

He heads to the kitchen to pour us drinks. When he returns with two large glasses of hetchwine I am naked, and playing the decastring on the sofa. He is agog.

I have not been given the knowledge of music before. The way my fingers flick across its strings, the technique of shifting a palm slightly to deaden the sound for effect, the resulting vibration across the hand; the glissandos, the trills; the chords dripping with feeling; the sheer *perfectness* of it, brings up an emotion I don't remember ever feeling. It is an upwelling, as if the biotech in my substrates is suddenly operating at double time. For a moment it is just me and the music in a vacuum of bliss. Everything disappears. The war. The target. My directive. Everything but these ten strings gently plucked, their wondrous music, and me and my fingers, effervesces from existence. I will never hear a sound more beautiful than this, whose name I do not even know.

The piece ends, and with surprise I realise I have shed a tear, and wonder why the factories even gave me that affectation. I quietly scan the datapack and find, with some disappointment, that he likes women who show emotion, as if he is attracted to the vulnerability he believes he lacks, and subconsciously seeks it out in others. The tear is automatic, a manipulation of melancholy. I feel anger for a moment.

I apologise and invent a story about my mother playing the same piece for me as a child.

"Don't be sorry, Essa…" (my substrates quiver at the sound of my name) "…that was beautiful. *Venthor's Requiem*. Fabulously difficult to play. And you played it perfectly. When did you learn? Here." He hands me the glass of hetchwine as I replace the decastring on the sofa.

Venthor's Requiem. I make a note never to forget it.

For a moment he seemed so entranced by my playing that he forgot I was naked. I sit confidently, my legs together, my back straight. He traces the lines of my tattoo with a finger. I conjure goosebumps for him. We each down our drinks, and I take him to the bedroom.

He doesn't even wonder how I already knew where it is.

As a lover he is gentle, but unconvincing in his gentleness. He makes love with a sort of reluctance, a lack of conviction. Like him, it is pleasant but ultimately disappointing.

That will change, I wager, in the unlikely event he ever fucks again.

His movements and rhythm are somehow disingenuous, as if he is acting as a selfless lover who cannot hide the fact that this pleasure is for him and him alone. He strokes my tattoo as we move together, and gradually his pace quickens, and quickens, and he can hide his selfishness no longer. I thank .Forum that it gives us the ability to feel pleasure. Though, I wonder if their pleasure is somehow different from ours, that there are feelings I will never feel no matter how well-designed our substrates and synapses are.

As he finishes, I think of *Venthor's Requiem*, and silently thank him; he is not the only one who has received a gift before he goes off to war.

I transmit the gene-program while he is still inside me. Like always, I feel a kind of turning in my stomach. It is not entirely unpleasureable.

As is standard, I spend the night. Half asleep, he muses about one day finding love.

When he wakes up, he complains of feeling unwell. He goes to the bathroom, grunting with pain. I quietly walk to the main room and get dressed. I sit down and play the decastring with distracted nonchalance as his moans of pain become guttural. Over the music, I hear him vomit.

"Essa!" Even in anger my name sounds beautiful.

He comes into the room. I stop playing. He is pale and sweating. His muscles quiver; already the gene-program is building new muscle, increasing bone density. His reflexes and senses will change soon.

I tell him not to be alarmed, that this is normal.

"Normal? *Normal?*" he screams. He stalks towards me, bent over, his shaking hands kneading his stomach. "What did you *do?* What have you *done to me?*"

I ask him to be calm. I apologise. He takes the decastring and hurls it against the wall. It explodes into pieces. Its strings break and twang horribly. I feel sadness.

The aggression components are already working on him. He will be a good soldier.

He turns from the ruined instrument. "You *bitch*, what have you done?"

I let him punch me three times before incapacitating him. I twist his arm on his fourth strike and with my other arm I chop at the nerve between shoulder and neck. He crumples, wailing.

His skin ripples. His screams of pain increase in intensity. He will not be moving from the floor for a few hours yet. I walk over to the smashed decastring, rend a piece in half, and put the little chunk of wood in my pocket.

I apologise again as I leave, though I'm not sure if it is to the decastring or the groaning, crumpled man becoming a killing machine on the floor of his apartment. .Forum will be watching, I tell him, in case anything goes wrong.

He screams after me as I close the door.

I awake on a gurney.

I sit up and look at myself in the mirror. I am about sixty years of age. Hair once black, now salt-and-pepper, slicked back; a pair of eyes whose wrinkles betray many years of laughter. I'm not in great shape. Little rolls of fat crease my belly, but she will forget about that, and concentrate on my smile and infectious laugh instead; the target is not a shallow woman.

I am a widower. I will be bewitched by her.

Essa lies on the gurney next to me, motionless, her eyes now silver-in-silver, washed out, the life literally gone from them.

"Goodbye, Essa," I say, and press the button. She disappears into the bowels of the Manufactory.

I find a piece of wood on the shelf in my locker, alongside other little trinkets and trophies. .Forum does not publicly allow this, but I suspect it turns a blind camera to my habit.

I dress. I walk through the halls of .Forum, humming *Venthor's Requiem*, and suddenly find the piece slightly annoying, shrill; a little gauche. An earworm I cannot shake. I shut it out, and eventually forget it.

I walk into the city a man.

Sometimes, What's Right in Front of You...

R V Neville

hat was that?

The washing machine was empty, it was definitely empty. This morning after its terminal hissy fit, Maeve had removed the wet sheets. She'd wrung the cloths, heavy with unspun water, out over the chipped bathtub and suspended them in the front room. Since the dryer had broken down last month, the rickety airer she'd seen in the flat when she'd viewed it in September had come into its own.

"That's one of the perks that comes with this place," the indifferent factor had told her, indifferently. There were plenty of other downwardly mobile people about, and he'd not tried to inveigle her.

So, what was the noise coming from the utility room? The *clang, clang, clang, kerbump* noises that the washing machine usually graced her otherwise-silent home with? She sauntered to the tiny room's door. Just as she peered round the doorframe, the racket stopped on a *clang*. She returned to her chair at the kitchen table and stared at her half-written article.

Like so many others, Maeve worked from home now. Only when she went on her 'woman-on-the-street' walks to scare up new stories for the papers, did she get out of the flat. The coffee and tea houses where she'd planned to write, to stay warm in deepest winter, were now closed. No one advanced a date for their reopening. The UFO sightings had seen to that.

Everyone had witnessed the lights. Millions saw the UFOs sweeping in from all sides. No one knew where they went. The people who could migrate had either made a dash for the countryside or a dash for the cities, trying to stay safe or trying to greet whatever came in the ships.

The sightings had shifted the world's economy in a matter of weeks. Only the most essential industries and businesses continued to operate. Governments everywhere said, "Stay inside. Stay quiet. Don't be a moving target." People lived at subsistence level. Those doing well were entrepreneurs who built new empires offering protection from, communication with, or speculation about who was in the UFO's.

All that fear. All that excitement. And no real telling if the things had landed or not.

Maeve hadn't the connections to thrive, so she gleaned tales at the raggedy parks, the near empty city square, the gull infested pier – the wee human-interest stories that people still wanted … no, *needed*, to read. Her most popular were about the dog found in a tree weeks after it went missing; the brave and desperate mother swinging her child at the playground; the flying saucer toy found in the park with no maker's name. She embroidered on most of her stories. The dog wasn't in a tree; the mother and child were real enough; and *she'd* been the finder in that last story, rather than her pathos-inviting invention of an old man who remembered the war.

But those were just fodder. What she needed was a real story to catapult her out of this morass her life had become. Something useful to her fellow human beings. Something to make her name.

She reached for the toy saucer, scraping at its resilient surface with her fingernail. When she'd first found it last month, it had sparkled with illumination, tiny lights winking on and off. She'd never found a battery compartment or a solar panel embedded in its smooth surfaces. Even now it sometimes blinked.

When the cafés had first closed, Maeve worried that someone, maybe the factor, maybe nosy old Mrs MacGillivray, would find her frozen to her chair one day in this close-view, north-facing flat.

Her relief was huge when she'd realised that by forgoing the price of a cup of coffee in the morning and a cup of tea in the afternoon, she was able to afford two whole extra hours of gas on the meter. That was double the hours she'd previously allowed herself. For four hours a day Maeve wasn't shivering or dressed up like Scott of the Antarctic. She sighed. Now that the washing machine had joined the dryer in retirement, she'd have to go to the laundrette. That meant more time in polar gear. Feck.

There it was again! *Clang, kerbump, clang, clang.*

This time, Maeve put the saucer down silently, then she rose slightly in her chair, clutched the seat with both hands and lifted it off the ground, still under her bum. She backed away, twirled the chair into one hand, then set it in place as if laying a lover to rest. She crossed the kitchen floor wraith-like, avoiding the squeaky tile midway. All the while, the washing machine continued its arrhythmic clanking.

When she reached the door, it stopped.

'Oh, *come* on!' Maeve stamped her foot and made to turn away again when something caught her eye.

The water lines that fed the washer rocked back and forth between the taps and where they disappeared behind the machine.

A warning bell clamoured in her head.

What was this?

Rats shoogling the lines? No, they'd moved out weeks ago in search of richer fare.

Poised between flight and fascination, Maeve let her breath seep from her mouth in a fine smoke-like stream. She watched as the rocking motion became more pronounced. When she took a step forward, the water lines halted as if frozen in the air. Breaking the silence, the machine juddered with so sudden a spasm of sound and motion that Maeve flinched.

Then, at much reduced decibels, it *kerbumped, clanged, clanged* again as if belching, politely. At the same time, its digital display started to flash hieroglyphic-like runes in place of numbers. In a moment of fierce recklessness Maeve took the second and final step that would bring her to the machine and snatched open the soap drawer.

There, long limbs folded in the main wash compartment, sat an olive-green man. Though 'man' might not be the right word: Being. Maeve and this Being stared at one another wide-eyed. Though, once again Maeve corrected herself. Its eyes were far taller than they were wide. Nevertheless, they stared at one another.

As she looked, the Being graded from olive to emerald. Not a chameleon then, or it would be dead white to match the drawer. A leprechaun? Stranger things had happened recently.

She whispered, "Who are you?"

The Being did not reply immediately but held up a tiny twinkling tablet in its hands. It tapped on the device, and a grumpy voice said, "Do you mean *you* can talk? We've only seen you moving about like herd animals. I've been trying to communicate with this creature for hours. I thought something was wrong with my programme!"

Maeve realised the 'creature' it spoke of was the washing machine. She narrowed her eyes, hands on hips, "Did you wrack my washer?"

RV Neville won the Constable Silver Stag Award (2020) for her first SF novel after gaining an MLitt from Dundee University (2019). Previously, she farmed organically while raising her family. She is now writing her second novel, a ghost story, set near her home by the shore of the Tay.

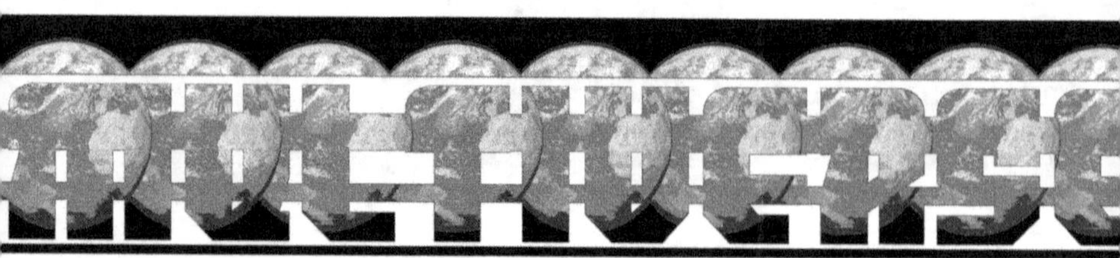

Solitude in Quotient

My parents injected me with math
when I was three –
for safety against the numbers;
the equations that didn't add up
for a generation, 'Quotient Free' as they
called it, a vaccine offering immunity
against a lifetime of even chances.

Disease had become solitude
in motion – perpetual exile of the
family unit; households limited
to two people, sharing two living areas,
not occupying less than two square metres;
isolation had become the cubed lifestyle,
a one parent to one child household.

Fractions were used to stem the
flow of appetite –
nutrition was a matter of proportions,
the two thirds filler diet; 'New Meat' redefined
the number of times you could divide a protein,
with stomach suppressors the food staple
for three fifths of the population.

Learning was now an aesthetic
lifestyle – the train travelling
away from the station by an accelerating
birth rate. If I finished school at eleven,
graduated college at fourteen, became a postgraduate
by sixteen, at what speed would I need to travel
to have a life?

Knowing there was no place
for me to share –
my parents taught me to add;
to keep counting until I was away
from a world's problems, this all added
to a binary seclusion; but in a world offering
no better chance, that's all numbers could provide.

Christopher Collingwood

Thought Experiment by Mathematica

The math gave awareness,
but the thought experiment was
too bold –
ego/quotient/absolute;
ambitious self-abstraction –
(virtuous calculate).
Imagining an equation
to define thought;
a calculation
to simulate personality –
(anima pura mathematica);
Identity divisible by –
psyche/axiom/logic;
an evolution deciphered
by unbound reason –
(natus ex arithmetica).
The student was asked
to surrender to a
defined awareness (pura numero),
(Self = computatio machina);
each breath becomes a number,
each thought an equation;
the mind, contestable by mechanics,
all provable by the will to try.
Concludi experimentum.

Christopher Collingwood

Chris was born and raised in Sydney Australia. He completed university in Sydney and graduated with a business degree. Chris has devoted his spare time to writing, with works published in *Neo-Opsis, Not One of Us, Liquid Imagination, Andromeda Spaceways, Abyss & Apex, Silver Blade*, and other dimensionally unstable anthologies.

Multiverse

an international anthology
of science fiction poetry

Includes "Embalmed" by Sofia Rhei, translated by Lawrence Schimel awarded winner of Best SF&F poem 2018

Come on a journey through time and space, viewing strange lives and meeting even stranger lifeforms from the darkest depths and brightest sparks of the imagination.

This landmark anthology, published in Scotland, includes more than 170 sci-fi poems by 70 contemporary writers from around the world, including Jane Yolen, Harry Josephine Giles, Sofia Rhei, Jenny Wong, James McGonigal, Fyodor Svarovsky, Joyce Chng, Vicente Luis Mora and Claire Askew.

£12.00, 234pp, paperback & £3.95 digital formats
Available in bookshops or from:

www.shorelineofinfinity.com

deline
Star Trek

Alex Storer meets Neil Cole

— the man with a

museum in his cellar

Few people can claim to have a museum in their cellar, but Neil Cole is one of them. I have followed Neil's endeavours for a few years, from the conversion of the cellar of his Grade II listed property into a vibrant museum (as seen on the Netflix series, *Amazing Interiors*), and at long last, I finally had the opportunity to visit. Nestled deep in the rolling hills of Northumberland, the picturesque town of Allendale is perhaps the last place one might expect to find a science fiction museum, yet it feels strangely at home. The Museum of Classic Sci-Fi is more than just a labour of love for its curator, it's a lifelong ambition.

As one might expect, a 300-year-old cellar does have its size limitations, but the sheer amount of film and television science fiction history that Neil has amassed in there is astounding. From the Dalek standing sentry outside the entrance, you'd be correct in assuming that the emphasis here is classic *Doctor Who* – but more on that later.

The first part of the museum features a wide range of items from film and television. Designed as a series of twisting corridors, from the moment you step through the doors, the walls are literally

'Madeleine'' mask from
Trek (2009). All photos:
Alex Storer

Alex Storer (right) with owner and curator of the
Museum of Classic Sci-Fi, Neil Cole (left)

lined with items from all eras. Starting with a replica of Robbie the
Robot from *Forbidden Planet* and items from *The Time Machine*, the
Museum begins with the early years of classic science fiction. As we
travel through the ages, you'll see masks, props, artwork, models and
costumes from the likes of the *Alien, Star Wars* and *Star Trek* franchises,
*Prometheus, Planet of the Apes, Babylon 5, Battlestar Galactica,
Blake's 7,* plus a wide range of items from the Marvel films.

The lighting evolves constantly through a spectrum of vibrant
colours, giving a special atmosphere to this Aladdin's Cave of treasures
and while there is a lot to see – all protected behind glass – it doesn't
feel cluttered. Neil takes pride in the authenticity of the collection;
most are screen-used items or production models, but he also makes
it perfectly clear where items have been restored or used in part with
replica elements. Everything is clearly labelled with supporting facts
and detail and in a nice personal touch, many exhibits are dedicated to
those who helped Neil realise this huge undertaking.

A Site for Thor's Thighs

Chris Hemsworth's screen-worn Thor armour from *The Avengers*,
John Shackley's oxygen suit from *The Tripods*, Kevin Bacon's *Hollow
Man* mask, Yori's original helmet from *TRON* and the Engineer from
Prometheus were among the standout items for me in the first section. I
still remember seeing *TRON* at the cinema and it has always been one
of my favourite films, so seeing just one small artefact from this piece of

cinema history was an unexpected surprise. Likewise, I loved the BBC's (sadly unfinished) adaptation of John Christopher's *Tripods,* so it was a real treat to see a rare surviving costume on public display for the first time.

Who's Doctor

A pair of iconic Police Box doors lead into the *Doctor Who* part of the museum, which was one of my main reasons for visiting. There hasn't been a permanent *Doctor Who* exhibition in the UK since the closure of the BBC's Doctor Who Experience in 2017 – and as time

Doctor Who: Props and costumes from the Tom Baker era plus Cyberman helmets from 1982's "Earthshock"

ticks on, the original props from the classic era of the show are both harder to come by and usually showing their age and fragility. Neil's long-standing passion for buying, restoring and preserving props and costumes from the series is testament to the impressive collection that follows, which our curator also views as an archive for these rare pieces of *Who* history.

The *Doctor Who* section makes up the bulk of the museum and chronologically explores all seven classic Doctors from 1963 to 1989. Alongside the exhibits, there is original artwork by Neil himself as

well as superbly rendered miniature dioramas making good use of the vintage Fine Art Casting models from the 1980s. On the subject of art, you'll also encounter various original pieces by *Who* illustration stalwart, Andrew Skilleter. You'll see a rare surviving Exxilon mask from 1974's *Death to the Daleks* and a range of costumes and weapons from the Tom Baker era, including *Warriors' Gate, The Brain of Morbius* and *Meglos*. Neil continues to add to the collection, with various items awaiting restoration or inclusion, such as a complete mummy head from the 1975 classic, *Pyramids of Mars*. One of the museum's current highlights is the full Zygon costume of Broton, from the 1975 story *Terror of the Zygons*. Kindly loaned to the museum by long-standing *Who* VFX guru Mike Tucker of The Model Unit, Broton looks fantastic and thanks to the creative lighting, just as terrifying as ever.

As we move into the 1980s, we see various relics from the Peter Davison era including Cybermen helmets and weapons from 1982's *Earthshock* alongside costumes from stories such as *Mawdryn Undead* and Davison's début, *Castrovalva*. Turning another corner, we find ourselves in perhaps the most impressive section, which features a wide range of complete monster outfits and other props and models. The fully-restored Terileptil costume from 1982's *The Visitation* looks stunning, alongside the enormous Garm from *Terminus*, who was lovingly restored to full glory by Neil.

Entering the Colin Baker era, another prop that was in a sorry state when he came into Neil's possession was Mestor, the large insect-like creature from 1984's *Twin Dilemma*. Thanks to Cole's craftsmanship, Mestor has never looked better. A surviving Cryon costume and seldom-seen black Cyberscout represent 1985's *Attack of the Cybermen*. Rarely exhibited items include a Tranquil Repose guard from *Revelation of the Daleks* and the T-Rex embryo from *Mark of the Rani*. I also spotted two items never previously displayed anywhere – the late Paul Darrow's costume from *Timelash* and an Arctic Haemovore from *The Curse of Fenric*.

A Dalek awaits as we turn the final corner into seventh Doctor territory, where props, costumes, models, masks and miniatures from the Sylvester McCoy years are displayed with exhibits from stories such as *Delta and the Bannermen, The Curse of Fenric* and *Time and the Rani*. Items like the Haemovour masks or the original exhibition replica of Kane's melted face and hands from 1987's *Dragonfire* provide a

Who: The original
costume from "Terror
Zygons" (1975)

Doctor Who: A fully restored red Terileptil costume and Terileptil mask from "The Visitation" (1982)

reminder of just how good the show's prosthetics and special effects were becoming at the point it was axed in 1989.

All too soon we're facing the (specially sculpted) exit door back out into the real world. Prints of Neil's vibrant artwork are available alongside as copies of the magazines specially produced for the museum's patrons, which take fascinating, in-depth looks at select items from the collection. While it's unlikely to get any bigger on the inside, the museum will evolve over time, as displays change and Neil's collection continues to expand.

The Museum of Classic Sci-Fi is a hidden gem and a real rarity. Whether you're a general fan of science fiction in film and television or if like me, you're an ardent *Doctor Who* obsessive, you will love Neil's collection, and it is an absolute joy to see so many items preserved and presented with such dedication. It's well worth the journey from wherever you're traveling.

You can find out more about the Museum of Classic Sci-Fi at https://www.museumofclassicsci-fi.com *or follow Neil's endeavours on Facebook:* https://www.facebook.com/neilcoleadventuresinscifimuseum/

Alex Storer is an artist, musician, graphic designer and occasional writer. Alex specialises in science fiction illustration, regularly working with authors and publishers. He also creates instrumental music under the name The Light Dreams.
You may have also worked out, he's a lifelong Doctor Who fan.
thelightdream.net
thelightdreams.bandcamp.com

Shards of Earth - Book I of the Final Architecture trilogy
Adrian Tchaikovsky
Tor
560 pages
Review by Jeffrey Palms

What might, in the wrong hands, be elevator-pitched as just another space opera starring a prefabbed complement of misfits (a cyborg, a test-tube baby, a few wayward humans, and for *Futurama* analogists even a crablike alien watchful of money) is, in fact, a paradigm-nudging masterpiece of worldbuilding, action, and tension. Admittedly, I had my doubts: from page one, you know you've signed up for a war-of-the-species plot greased together by a starjumping gang of "spacers," each threatening to be a little more Han Solo than the last.

Could it really anchor my attention for half-a-thousand pages?Thank goodness I picked up *Shards of Earth*. Not only is it un-put-downable and damn near flawless, but it *does* engage with the social zeitgeist, and in cleverly understated ways. All the spacefaring thrills of interspecies war are underpinned by a writerly intelligence that I just don't associate with the subgenre, and, well – you couldn't ask for a pleasanter surprise.

To the book, then. `Something out there is hunting intelligent life in the universe, humankind included. The something are moon-sized aliens that travel though "unspace," a kind of fabric that exists underneath the real; they can turn up in a star system unheralded, ready to deal planetary deathblows. As cool as that is, it's also fascinating: the aliens exist on a scale entirely different to humankind. Their size, age, and mind cannot be fathomed, and even Idris Telemmier, the "intermediary" of the circle of protagonists who alone is cranially equipped to do primitive business with these giants, can only stab into their minds for painful moments at a time. The way these uncanny hunters cannot be mentally reckoned with in one shot, or even seen at one time – hanging as they do half in unspace – makes me think a little bit of Timothy Morton's hyperobjects, at least in an atmospheric sense: they're glimpsable and real, but fundamentally unknowable. Like global warming.

In keeping with the menacing aspect of such a mysterious power, the novel's present-day plot is founded on a moment seventy years earlier when one of these alien giants, known as Architects, destroyed Earth – which it did by turning our planet into an austere, gorgeous, lifeless *sculpture*. Reason: totally unknown.

Thus severed from the Earth, humanity now exists only in a periphery of other worlds and amongst a plethora of bedfellows. In its backdrop, then, the book trades in a humanity that cannot but exist on the toes of some *other*: they have to live on planets that aren't Earth, fly on ships navigated by biologically altered pilots, vie with aliens of all stripes, negotiate with parahumans. Add to that the existential threat of an incomprehensibly complex and disinterested killing force, and you've got a bizarrely familiar rendering of the age we live in, the least preachy Anthropocene I think I've yet encountered. Not that preachiness on that topic is always bad, and Tchaikovsky's engagement with it certainly takes a backseat to his plotted action – but this is worldbuilding of an amazing order. It's like sitting on a butt-pillow designed by I.M. Pei.

By the start of the novel the Architects have gone, thanks to some long-past heroics on the part of Idris, who has since put himself out to pasture as the navigator for a salvaging crew that drags in valuable junk from deep space. He's too universe-weary for anything but this freelance arrangement, still bitter from the government programmes that used him and, in their wartime pursuits, let some of his classmates die.

Then – fairly foreseeable but necessary as a matter of course

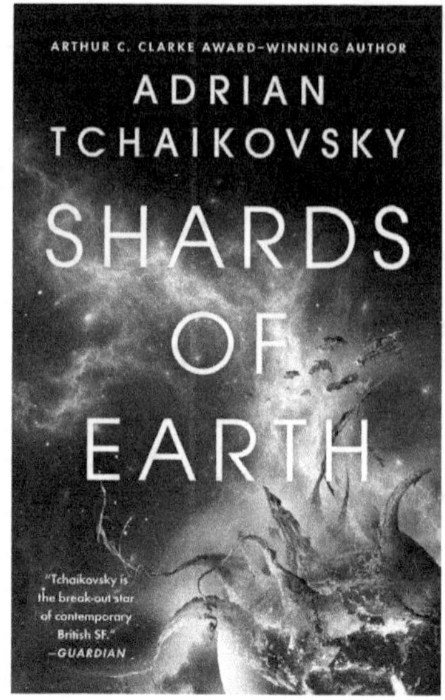

– during a routine job, Idris and his crewmates aboard the *Vulture God* discover a ship that has been sculpted with the signature artistry of the moon-sized monsters. It seems that the Architects are back. The nightmare is reigniting. This sets off the rest of the book's action, and I dare say the rest of the trilogy's action, which is rendered episodically: you have the question of whether the sculpted ship is a hoax; gunfights with alien gangsters; the rescuing of a Hiver academic from a mysterious comms-jamming planet; the horrors of unspace; and so on.

Certain of the prolonged action scenes did induce some attention-glazing, I will say, but only because they took me away from the narrative's wheelhouse: Tchaikovsky's ability to draw individualized characters against a backdrop of highly credible and recognizable geopolitical factions, each of them pushed to a colour-showing fore by the news of the returned Architects.

How these intergalactic politics are rendered through characters and dialogue and not via chapter-long info-dumps is some kind of sausage-making magic I don't want to see, but on the reader side it's pure delight.

This latter observation is a triumph of craft that, even alone, probably does make the 560-page trek worthy of attempt; but where *Shards* truly delivers is unspace and the Architects. This is existential horror in thoughtfully modern clothing, the Death Star's nuclear holocaust reworked as environmental terror. It's zippy in its action but appropriately slow-mo in its revelation of dread.

Can't wait for Part II.

The Magic Fix
Mark Montanaro
Elsewhen Press, 256 pages
Review by Samara Wright

The world of *The Magic Fix* has a lot of the elements of a fantasy; Trolls, Goblins, Ogres, Pixies, Elves, Humans, magic, a quest, and a dragon. Yet, I struggle to classify it as strictly fantasy. There's plenty of comedy, political maneuverings, and a mysterious assassination. *The Magic Fix* is a little bit of everything.

We begin the story in the aftermath of a devastating battle between the Humans and the Trolls. The Humans are losing, and without help, they may just need to concede defeat. Plans are set in motion: the King sets off to ask aid from their allies, the Elves; one of the King's counsel secretly puts a plan into action to end the war; the Ogres plot to assassinate the Goblin King; and a Pixie discovers she has power the likes of which have never been seen in all of the Known World.

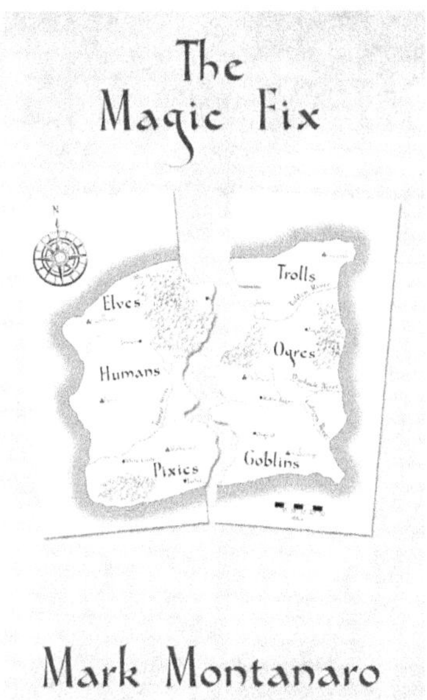

The writing is fast-paced and lighthearted. We never get bogged down in the details of the world, history or lore. I would even say that the world-building was lacking. We are thrown into this fantasy world, complete with a map, but barely get any information on anything, outside of what the author could twist into a humorous exchange.

The dialogue is where Montanaro really shines; it's funny and often sarcastic, but never loses the easy-going, quick-read feel of the rest of the book. The plot was confusing at times. Distances and travel times varied and the sarcastic comments within each character's inner monologues could be distracting. We jump from a quest to kill the Goblin King to a murder mystery who-dun-it, without a satisfactory conclusion to either.

Without giving anything away, the end of the book for some characters felt triumphant and wrapped up their storylines neatly while others were left in limbo. If the author is planning for a sequel, there's plenty of potential in where the book ended, but I would have liked a few more chapters or even another entire act to see what happens to the rest of the ensemble cast.

If you enjoy character driven fantasy, *The Magic Fix* is a quick, easy read, perfect for a lazy weekend.

Switch
A.S. King
Dutton Books for Young Readers
240 pages
Review by Veronika Groke

Switch is a novel directed at teen and young adult readers by acclaimed American author A.S. King.

On one level, *Switch* is an intriguing exploration of family dysfunction and what it means to be 'normal': overshadowed by the absence of her mother and the legacy of her psychotic sister's abuse, Tru's family lives in a house whose insides have been entirely covered in plywood by their safety-obsessed father. The father, an electrician, looks at the world as an assemblage of circuits and switches, of energy that must be contained in order for his family to be safe. The way he does this is to box them all in in layers upon layers of plywood to keep them away from the electrics in the walls, including the eponymous Switch, of which not even the father knows what it will do if flicked. As a result, Tru has to constantly counteract her father's safety measures if she and her brother Richard don't want to be completely shut in.

Exacerbating the father's anxiety is the long shadow cast by Tru and Richard's now-absent sister, whose cruelties were not only directed at family members directly but also consisted in playing one out against another, and whose sneakily planted 'bombs' the family keep setting off unexpectedly. The most urgent problem, however, appears to be the absence of the mother, an amateur psychic, whose unexplained departure nine months previously caused the father to quit his job — and, it appears, stopped time.

This is where, unfortunately, the story is undermined by being squeezed into an inherently flawed conceptual framework, in which time is said to have stopped (or been stopped by someone), but everything nonetheless stays the same: 'Our hair grows / babies are born / people die. But time has stopped.' An artificial 'Solution Time' is invented, measured by a mechanism called 'N3WCLOCK', which tells people what time and date it would be if time hadn't stopped. What remains unclear throughout, however, is in what ways exactly Solution Time is meant to differ from 'real time', seeing as how nothing has otherwise changed. This unclear state of affairs inevitably leads to internal contradictions, as when Tru, the narrator, muses that she wants 'time to start moving again so we don't always have to spend our free time thinking about solutions'.

The youngest in her family, Tru is a high school student who spends most of her not-really-time hanging out with her group of friends in the 'Psych Team' trying to find a real solution for the alleged time problem. (For some also unexplained reason, this task has been allocated to high schoolers.) Again, the interactions between the Psych Team's members, and the evolving dynamics of their relationships, are well-observed and well-written, but, like the father's box constructions, are overlayered by the ever-increasing implausibility of the 'time problem', which is expressed in an overabundance of disconnected themes and mixed metaphors that read more like notes for a story than an actual story.

Hailed by some critics as a surrealist masterpiece, I confess that, to me, *Switch* reads like a not entirely successful attempt at experimental writing by an otherwise very skilled author with more ideas than would fit into one short novel. B3RTRAND RUSS3LL / is lit on fire / with Palaeolithic / energy / to think outside the box / give a shit / don't give a shit / you can't make things make sense just by repeating them. This explanation will do.

Cover Story: Mike Holzinger, aka Hap N Stance

Noel Chidwick

I love watching videos of flythroughs in simulated space, and I enjoy listening to (and creating) electronic music of the more spacey kind, so I was delighted to come across this video by Hap N Stance:

This is not only beautiful to watch, but also to listen to, accompanied as it is by the music of Alex Storer of Light Dreams. Time for a break from editing duties.

Except the editorial brain does not switch off. At around one minute in, my thought was: this'd make a stunning cover for Shoreline of Infinity. I wonder...

A little email chase via Alex Storer, and I managed to make contact with Hap n Stance, whose name in RealSpace is Mike Holzinger. A few exchanges, and yes, Mike would be delighted for us to use a frame for the front cover. And that is what you are holding in your hands.

Keen to find out more about how Mike makes his films I asked him a few questions

NC: *Mike, tell us a little about yourself and what you do.*

MH: I am a retired meteorologist, having worked for the U.S. National Weather Service.

Science fiction, space art, and astronomy have always been an interest of mine. Isaac Asimov's Foundation series is my favorite sci-fi. I am a member of the International Association of Astronomical Artists, and the Denver Astronomical Society. I am using the universe simulator Space Engine to make You Tube videos.

I post still images from Space Engine on Twitter @hapnstance1. Most of my videos use music by the artist and musician Alex Storer of The Light Dreams.

 NC: *What inspired you into making these videos?*

MH: I am not a high-tech guy, but saw an excellent YouTube video from someone who used Space Engine [the software and graphics tool for creating these interstellar flythroughs]. I said to myself, "I have to learn how to do that", and did it.

NC: *How easy is for for folk to learn how to make their own tours of the Universe, and how do they get started?*

MH: Anybody can do it, but there is a learning curve. First, you need a fairly powerful computer to run Space Engine. Second, you need to learn how to navigate in Space Engine. It is mostly trying it out and experimenting, but there is an online manual, including a "Flight School". Third, record what you are doing, and compile it into a video.

Excuse me, I'm off to travel through the Universe...

Links:

Mike's videos: https://www.youtube.com/c/HapNStance/videos — indulge yourself

Space Engine: http://spaceengine.org - you too can fly through space.

Alex Storer's website: https://thelightdreams.wordpress.com/ — This is the same Alex Storer who provide two stunning covers for our summer issues, and also the report on the Classic Sci-Fi Museum. Alex is a busy, multi-talented Being.